POLITICAL

(being an annotated illustrated pamphlet
of Common Sense)

Howard Richard Debs

*I think artist and activist is the same thing.
As artist, you always have to be an activist.
I think every art, if it's relevant, is political.
—Ai Weiwei, dissident Chinese artist*

Cover photo by author taken July 2015. "At the window" Rose Hill Mano Frederick, Maryland; the retirement home of Thomas Johnson, the first elected Governor of the State of Maryland and Associate Justice of the United States Supreme Court. It was built in the mid-1790s. For notes and reflections regarding this and the other images included, all by the author unless otherwise credited, as well as supplemental material related to the
work in general please visit the author's website
https://howarddebs.com/

Cyberwit.net
HIG 45 Kaushambi Kunj, Kalindipuram
Allahabad - 211011 (U.P.) India
http://www.cyberwit.net
Tel: +(91) 9415091004 +(91) (532) 2552257
E-mail: info@cyberwit.net

Printed at Thomson Press India Limited.

*For my daughters, Alissa and Lauren, who
exemplify caring*

Acknowledgments

Many thanks to the following literary journals where these poems first appeared, sometimes in earlier versions.

Former People Journal: "Custer's Last Stand" and "An All-American Anecdote" and "Weed/Killer" as "Political: An Annotated Illustrated Trilogy"

The Bees Are Dead: "Fundamental Attribution Error"

Poets Reading the News: "Waypoints" and "Real Fake News" and "On Reading About The Lost Poetry Of The Angel Island Detention Center"

Inkstain Press: "The Cynic"

Social Justice Poetry: "Payday Lender Customer Briefly Seen On TV"

New Verse News: "The Conspiracy Surrounding The 2016 Word Of The Year"

Tuck Magazine: "Drumbeat" and "The Thimble Is Gone, What Next?" and "Before Hanukkah, 2018"

Verse-Virtual: "Indigenous" and "All American" first published in *Florida English Journal*

Unlikely Stories: "Survival Of The Fittest"

Thank you to Emily Jo Scalzo for your assistance with and generous comments about this work. For her insightful contribution regarding the background and merits of chapbooks, thank you to Nellie Pierce. Thank you to Robbi Nester for her review of Nellie's contribution. I thank Shauna Makrealeas for her review and advice regarding the image content. My gratitude to Dr. Karunesh Kumar, Managing Editor and all associated with Cyberwit.net for your dedication to the literary arts. And to my wife Sheila, thank you for everything.

Contents

"A Living History of the Chapbook—and Beyond"
by Nellie Pierce

If modern democracy owes its birth and sustenance to the cheap, decentralized, and unhindered exchange of information, then the chapbook is its form par excellence. By its example, we may observe that the power of literacy comes in small packages—whether these be bits, or duodecimo bindings.

Before an explosion of letterpress technology catapulted 16th century Europe into what Marshall McLuhan once termed "the Gutenberg galaxy," books had long been the preserve of the wealthy. This changed, however, when the increasing accessibility of paper and printing presses made it feasible for unbound books of eight or twelve pages to be sold for a penny or less—not as negligible a price as it may seem today, but still, within reach of the average day-laborer's wages. Itinerant peddlers called "chap-men" arose to meet this demand, carrying printed matter from presses in the cities to an eager audience of the rural working classes. These early readers thrilled to tales of adventure and roguery. Even those who couldn't read were able to participate, thanks to the chapbook's fluid relationship with orality: many early examples came in the form of folk songs, meant to be performed publicly as well as read in private. Early chapbooks also tended to be profusely illustrated, but this wasn't always an aid to comprehension—because woodcut engravings were so cheap to reproduce, they were often recycled throughout many different texts with little regard for the subject matter.

Chapbooks' wide accessibility made them a political force to be reckoned with. Literacy rates burgeoned among the European public in the late 17th century, abetted by the institution of charity schools for educating the poor, but also likely owing to the sheer abundance of printed matter. In any case, whether they merely responded to the demands of an increasingly literate public, or played a part in producing it, the rise of chapbooks accompanied an unprecedented state of affairs: reading was no longer the sole domain of the upper classes.

This might not have been so disruptive if the form were restricted to folk tales and ballads, but by the 18th century, some chapbooks began to reflect the Enlightenment mores that were taking society by storm. Examples include Thomas Paine's The Rights of Man, which was copiously reprinted in chapbook form for years after its publication in 1791. The insurrectionary potential of pamphlets like Paine's inspired a backlash. Increasingly stringent applications of copyright law, as well as injunctions against public solicitation, helped to put a damper on the chapman's trade. While chapbooks had originally sprung up to appeal to their audience's unstudied interests, relating their stories in an amoral and non-didactic tone, publishers in the 19th century began to prescribe certain interests to their readers for their own good. This led to a proliferation of religious chapbooks, often called "Sunday schools" or "godlinesses," which aimed to bolster the moral fiber of the plebeian masses whom the racier strand of chapbooks had previously entertained.

This sanctimonious turn ushered in a long period of dormancy. Along the way, chapbooks lost their monopoly on the dissemination of cheap print: industrialization reduced the costs of printing once again, allowing lower class readers to lift their sights from the compact octavo or duodecimo bindings of the traditional chapbook towards the sprawling forms of newspapers and novels. By the time the chapbook returned, in the early 20th century, it was to bear the evidence of these radical changes.

At the time of its resurgence, the term "chapbook" may have been a conscious archaism hearkening back to a preindustrial past. The printing press enjoyed a rush of renewed interest beginning in the late 19th century, thanks to the Arts and Crafts movement—a group of artists and designers who reacted to what they saw as the garish aesthetic standards of the day by advocating a return to traditional methods of handicraft.

Chapbooks, which began their history spurred by the early forerunners of industrial technologies, now arose in protest to the alienation thought to be inherent in mass production. Along with this stylistic shift came a major reorientation in genre: where the chapbooks of yore focused on the episodic and the epic, tales of daring and debauchery, the new artisanal chapbook adopted a lyric mode. Its primary genre was poetry.

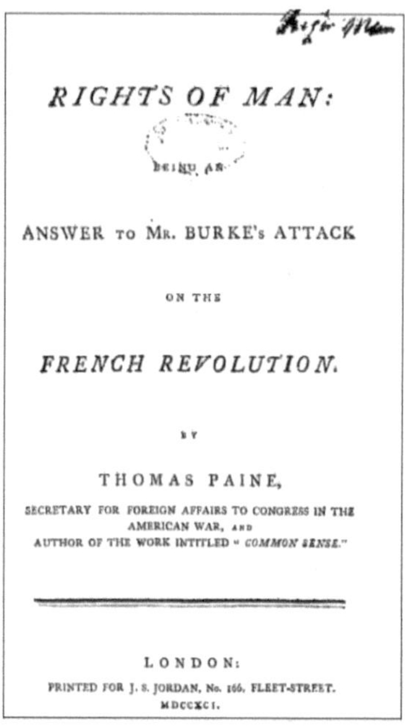

Rights of Man title page from the first edition, 1791

At first this meant the poetry of the early Modernists—writers like H.D., T.S. Eliot, and Djuna Barnes—who published short-form leaflets of their work, as well as placing it in collections and literary magazines. It also saw currency with Dadaists in Europe, and in the tracts of the Russian avant-garde. But the chapbook maintained its ambivalent relationship with the aesthetics and distribution methods of high and low culture. Soon the 20th century brought its own technological changes, in the form of typewriters and mimeograph machines that put the means of textual reproduction more directly in the hands of writers than ever before. Among others, the Beat poets of the 1950s seized eagerly upon these tools. The utilitarian manuscripts they hacked out of their typewriters may seem a far cry from the nostalgic designs of Arts and Crafts printers like William Morris, but there is some coherence to this unlikely pedigree. The creators of chapbooks have always been concerned with circumventing the official channels by which writing is allowed to make itself available to a public. Over the course of the 20th century, this labor was to unite authors as disparate as feminist consciousness raising groups and Star Trek fans, as the chapbook morphed into the zine.

With the dawn of the new millennium, these new standard-bearers were empowered by digital media to broadcast their various gospels yet more expediently, and further. In the days of the early Internet, the vector might be a blog or personal website. Collective knowledge projects such as Wikipedia and The Internet Archive also carried forward the tradition of making printed (and other) information as widely available as possible. Some of these techno-utopian stirrings have, arguably, since yielded to a similar logic as shooed away the chapman: in contrast to the pure DIY ethos of zine mailing lists, or the peer-to-peer listservs and chatrooms that descended from them, most of content shared on the internet today passes through the pipeline of social media platforms. Repudiating some of the liabilities of authorship--but nonetheless retaining rights to skim off the choicest cream from every crop of "user-generated content"—such platforms outsource the means of mass reproduction, while they raise questions concerning free speech, data ownership, and the relation between public good and private profit. They also restore to our social world an animate quality scarcely known since the genesis of print culture: when news is spread by shaky cell-phone video as often as it is by dry report, and opinions are just as readily expressed by absurdist image templates as they are by argument, we seem to near a referendum on the norms, and purposes, of discourse. Can the affordances of our technological moment support a radically new and increasingly egalitarian relation between individuals and the communicative means to which they have access? Or must we entertain one of McLuhan's darker theses: is there room for the democratic way of life in our imploded world?

To these doubts, we may find no answer but the solace of indeterminacy. The heirs to the chapbook tradition multiply as fast as do their media: they are no less to be found in viral images than they are in discursive podcasts—in antiracist infographics as much as in conspiratorial screeds—in crowdfunded video essays no more than in

YouTube make-up tutorials—and in trending hashtags perhaps more visibly, but no more authentically, than in small press poetry publications. All of these media proliferate possible futures. Thus, one might wish to echo the warning with which William Carlos Williams concludes his "Asphodel, That Greeny Flower:" "It is difficult/to get the news from poems/yet men die miserably every day/for lack/of what is found there." The juncture at which we find ourselves urges daring hybrids. The dream of a truly democratic media culture may—or may not—perish, for want of the attempt.

*Adapted from the article "A Very Short History of the Chapbook" originally published by the author as a Postgraduate Fellow in the blog of Middlebury College Library, Special Collections, December 2018.

Custer's Last Stand

FADE IN:

INT. FARMHOUSE LIVING ROOM - EVENING
Farm near Two Rivers Wisconsin, Summer rain falling, Custer and his wife Molly have finished dinner and are watching Fox News on TV

                    CUSTER
          There's no doubt about it, they're finally
          gonna make everything all right
          again.

                    MOLLY
          It sure has taken 'em long enough.

                    CUSTER
I'm just glad they're doin' what they
promised. We did our part, things couldn't
keep goin' this way, it was gettin'
worse by the day. This is just the start,
once this healthcare thing is done
they'll make headway on infrastructure,
taxes, you'll see.

                    MOLLY
And that new plant they just announced
They're gonna build down in Kenosha,
that Asian company, lots of new jobs,
it's just what we hoped for.

                    CUSTER
Any more of your delicious pie left
from last night?

                    MOLLY
On top of the fridge, in the
Tupperware container.

                              CROSSFADE:

INT. FARMHOUSE LIVING ROOM LATER

                    CUSTER
                 (agitated)
I don't know what's goin' on,
some kind of procedural thing.
They better move this along,
it's gettin' late. All I know
is we gotta give people back
their rights, nobody tells me
what to do. I'm sick and tired

of it, get off people's backs,
come on, let's get this done.

          MOLLY
Calm down. It'll be fine.

          CUSTER
Nobody ever gave us a handout.
We been breakin' our backs all
our lives. People gotta get back
to hard work, no favors. That's
what this country's all about.
Pull yourself up by your own
bootstraps, fend for yourself.

          CROSSFADE:

INT. FARMHOUSE LIVING ROOM LATER

          CUSTER
What the hell, I can't believe
it, they couldn't get the votes
to pass the damn thing. Now what's
gonna happen? The bastards!

          MOLLY
I guess we're never gonna get back
to the way it was.

          CUSTER
I'll be damned! The Mexicans,
the Muslims, Transgender, what
the hell, they're gonna take over.
This is a different country than I
grew up in, it's not my country
anymore, what are we gonna do now?

          FADE OUT.

          THE END

On July 28, 2017 my wife and I sat riveted by the proceedings surrounding the so-called skinny repeal vote regarding The Affordable Care Act. We witnessed as history unfolded. It was like watching a movie. The "thumbs-down" of the late Senator John McCain doomed the bill. After the vote failed, both the Majority and Minority Senate leaders spoke about those on the other side of the aisle. It is always about the other. I have thought considerably about the other couple sitting somewhere in mid-America, the rust belt, watching as did we, and wondering what it all might mean from where they sit. This 'hybrid' work, uses the 'form' of scriptwriting to create a poetic statement. I have used the formatting there employed. In my writing in general I subscribe to the considerations suggested by Denise Levertov relating to her conception of organic form. When tussling with the subject matter involved in this instance, it became clear dialog was called for and the framework of a script was not only apt but necessary. I took the accompanying photo not far out from Cleveland, an area similar to the farmland surrounding the Two Rivers community where the action in this piece takes place, and all of this section of our nation is alternately known as the "Rust Belt" and "Flyover Country"

An All-American Anecdote

While savoring breakfast at my favorite local diner a burly African American customer without being asked, on his way to the cashier to pay seeing a disabled Caucasian American having no success being transferred from his seat to his wheel chair by his wife, then further aided by two waitresses to no avail, that person helped move the patron in need, all involved matter-a-factly acknowledging each other, and bidding all a fine day, the good Samaritan went on his way, restoring my faith in the real America on display.

I am a devotee of the all-American diner. It is a bulwark in the fabric of this country. I have taken countless photos of diners as I have occasioned upon them in my travels and lauded the institution in my paean "The Yankee Diner" featured in the publication Jewish Currents and my book Gallery: A Collection of Pictures and Words. I find all I need to know within the confines of these establishments, and I consider the prose poem recitation of this observation as a form of bearing witness. I took the accompanying photo, an authentic restored classic diner, a Worcester #787 Streamliner, originally built in 1946, while traveling through in August of 2005 in Quechee Vermont, near the Quechee Gorge known as "The Little Grand Canyon of New England." A real diner is truly "the people's house."

Weed/Killer (a found poem)

It's an agonizing death,
dying of non-Hodgkin's lymphoma
in his case
claimed to be caused
by Monsanto's Roundup
used by the school
groundskeeper.
In the opening statement
of the trial
his attorney shows
photos of the lesions
on his client's body.
The groundskeeper
read the label
contacted the company
after developing a rash

was never warned
it could cause cancer,
so he maintains.
Monsanto's counsel
tells the jury it takes
years for the disease
to develop, that the
cancer started well
before the groundskeeper
started working in the schools.
Glyphosate, the suspect ingredient
is safe, shown by numerous studies
so states Monsanto's counsel in
delivering his opening statement.
The World Health Organization
has classified the ingredient
as a probable human carcinogen.
California has added the ingredient
to its list of chemicals known
to cause cancer.
The EPA says glyphosate
is safe for humans
when used according
to the directions on the label.
A federal judge in Sacramento
blocked the state of California
from requiring Roundup to carry
a warning. "The simple fact is
he is going to die.
It's just a matter of time,
between now and then
it's just nothing but pain"
so pleads the attorney
for the plaintiff.

"how is it to be told? . . . in detailing the facts themselves?" This statement comes from the Reznikoff Papers housed at the University of Arizona, Box VII, Folder 26. Charles Reznikoff, was a member of a small group of poets known as objectivists and is a virtual mentor of mine. Holocaust, all 94 pages of it, was published in 1975, and was Reznikoff's found poetry tour de force. The work uses actual testimony (Reznikoff had a law degree) extracted from 26 volumes of transcriptions from the court proceedings of the Eichmann and Nuremberg trials. Pondering the AP story about the Monsanto case elicited a poetic concern for the prospects at the most human level for a country whose judicial, legislative, and executive branches collectively abandon support of its citizenry, favoring profit (kleptocracy) over protection of the individual. Subsequent to the writing of this found poem jurors decided the case in favor of the plaintiff awarding him $289 million in damages. I took the accompanying photo of the field of sunflowers at a vintage restoration area in New Hampshire. The sunflower is a kind of cousin to the dandelion which is most often incorrectly considered a weed. Up until the 1800s dandelions were seen as extremely beneficial. People would remove grass to plant dandelions. It's all the way you look at it. Source: AP article July 9, 2018 "First trial over Roundup weedkiller cancer claim under way"

Fundamental Attribution Error

I don't want to be an alarmist but around the corner outside of this library in an alcove near the emergency exit there's a good-sized chartreuse suitcase just lying on its side and people are passing by ignoring it; I saw it on my way in to return my books, it's there next to a large plastic bag stuffed full, I'm not sure what's inside the bag or the suitcase either so I thought I'd better let someone know oh you're saying it's someone who's homeless, who left them there to come inside to cool off, they do it all the time Ok so I'll leave it up to you to decide what to do I didn't intend to cause a scare but you can't be too careful nowadays, with so many crazy people out there you know what I mean.

Waypoints

Maumee is 17 minutes
(10.3 miles) from Toledo
    the highways intersecting there
    known as the Crossroads
    of America
via the Anthony Wayne Trail
    named after the Revolutionary
    War general known as "Mad Anthony"
it is 8 hours 11 minutes
(543.6 miles) from Charlottesville
    named in honor of Princess Charlotte,
    who became queen of England when
    she married King George the Third
    known as the "mad king who lost America"

via I-80 East and I-76
Get on I-80 East/I-90 East/Ohio Turnpike
from Conant Street head north
Continue onto South Reynolds Road
Use the right lane to take
Interstate 80/Interstate 90/Ohio Turnpike ramp
Keep right at the fork, follow signs
for I-90 East/I-80/Cleveland
> *a terminus of the Underground*
> *Railway used by slaves to reach*
> *free states during the Civil War*

merge onto I-80 East/I-90 East
Follow I-80 East and I-76
take Ohio Turnpike past Akron
> *once known for fastest growing city*
> *in the U.S. also known for Addie Polk,*
> *who shot herself while being evicted*
> *during the U.S. foreclosure crisis*

Head past Youngstown
> *nestled in the Mahoning Valley region*
> *which thrived on coal and steel, now part*
> *of the Rust Belt, immigrant incursions*
> *sparked major Ku Klux Klan activity*
> *there in the Roaring Twenties*

Pass by Pittsburgh
> *"the Steel City" heralded as the*
> *"arsenal of democracy" during*
> *World War II producing 95 million*
> *tons for the war effort*

Keep following I-76 south
> *60 miles southeast of Pittsburgh*
> *is the 9/11 Flight 93 National Memorial*

Take exit 161 for I-70 East toward US-30/Breezewood/Baltimore
> *Baltimore shed blood in 1861 with the*
> *first deaths of the Civil War, in 1968*
> *after the King assassination, again in 2015*
> *following the death of Freddie Gray*

Stay with I-81 towards Harrisonburg
>*bastion of diversity in the Shenandoah Valley*
>*high schoolers there speak 55 languages in*
>*addition to English, proud to be the place of origin*
>*for the multilingual yard sign "Welcome Your Neighbors"*

Follow I-81 South and I-64 East

Take exit 221 for I-64 East toward Richmond
>*capital of the commonwealth, known among other things*
>*as the place at which was passed the Virginia Statute for*
>*Religious Freedom written by Jefferson himself*

Take exit 121B to merge onto VA-20 North toward Charlottesville
arrive at intersection of
Fourth and Water streets
Recalculating . . .

I thought about the passage to Charlottesville taken by the perpetrator in the killing by car of Heather Heyer. The probable route represents America, its history, and along the way there are to be found signposts indicating directions, for good or ill, we have taken as a nation. This tragic occurrence now brings us to yet another point along the way. Where we are next heading is yet to be determined. VA-20, the last leg of the route to Charlottesville in this poem is called "The Constitution Route." It was so designated by the Virginia legislature in 1976. The route encompasses the National Scenic Byway that passes by the homes of three of America's Founding Fathers and presidents. It is part of National Geographic's "Journey through Hallowed Ground."

The Cynic

I'm a hundred
and one
I've seen
everything
that can be done,
here in Beantown
where I come from.
Talk about your
son of a bitch politicians
there's a line
as long as your arm.
Curley goin' back to the 30s,
White who ran against
Louise Hicks back in '67,
or was that '66? A woman
ain't no different.
My old pa used to say
if things keep goin' this way
they'll run out of candidates
one fine day!
Will Rogers had it right,
he said somethin' like
if you put truth into
politics you'd have
no politics.
Now they've sure got a
lot this time around;
it's a great pissin' contest
that's for sure
but we're the real
losers as usual
sucker punched by a
bunch of sneaky petes.
It don't matter if you're
Democrat, Republican, or
Independent, all politicians
are just plain crooked.

Baltimore Mom Proves Violence Is America's Answer

It starts once more on these streets. Bloodshed in
Baltimore took turns in 1812 against *that* conflict,
again in 1861, when the first deaths of *that* Civil War
came on *that* battleground, in 1968 after the King
assassination and now this latest chapter
of dread gone on a rampage goes into the
record book, along with the mom that stole
America's heart and soul caught on video gone viral
in the throes of violence against her own son.
What does Twitter America have to say?
"To the mom who caught and beat her son
in the street for rioting, you're a damn good parent,
you go lady." "[Watch the] video of #Baltimore mom
after finding her son rioting; [see her] slapping sense into him."
"This mom is the best." "[This mom is] mom of the year."
"She showed that mudder fukker (sic) kid."
Mothers of America, this is another *Answer*
grab his hand and hold it to your heart and beg him
to come with you. Say you feel unsafe and
you need him to come with you to protect you;
if you plead and beg and he still moves
towards *that* flame, let him go.

---

*One of my two adult daughters, now a mother herself, not the one
who teaches autistic children who I am very proud of as well, the one
who is an LCSW, posted on FB a counter position statement to that
circulating about the Baltimore mom who tried using physical force
with her son to get him to do the right thing during the riots that
occurred there at the time. She wrote in part: "I understand why
everyone is posting and applauding the Baltimore mom who is shown on
video attempting to remove her son from the riots, but I find it baffling*

that no one is mentioning her own violent behavior. She is hitting and beating up her son. Caught in the moment or a cycle of family violence that leads her son to believe violence is the answer? Family violence is a core issue in our society and contributes to the high rate of violent crime in our communities. Kids are not only abused but disciplined in ways that promote the notion that violence is a path to problem solving. We are saying violence is not the right path to protest injustice, and yet people are lifting this woman up who is acting out violently towards her son. I applaud her passion to get him to not act out, I feel for her as a mom and know she only wanted to protect her child from the current events unfolding, but I cannot applaud her method. In many ways, she is part of the problem."

Payday Lender Customer Briefly Seen On TV

Good evening, I'm Harriet
Ashbury your roving reporter at WNTV
and I'm standing here in the middle
of this establishment talking to people
waiting in line to take out loans against
their next paycheck. The new Consumer
Financial Protection Bureau has
just proposed regulations for
these types of short term small loans
and we want to find out what those
who use these think. So your name is?

Shelly.

Have you been to this place before?

Oh, yes, many times, I'm here
to refinance and get $150 now to pay the rent
it's due before my next paycheck goes through.

Where do you work?

I'm at Burger Bob's
mostly in the back doin' fries.

How much do you
earn if you don't mind my asking?

I make eight bucks an hour, they have me work
30 hours, so they don't pay no benefits;
my mom, she can't work has a bad back, she takes
care of my two little girls so I can be at BB's, so it's
hard making it through each week
with groceries, rent, you know what I mean.

Where's your husband? Do you have a husband?

He left me, he drank pretty much. It's better he's gone.

Where do you live? Tell me about where you live.

We live at the Acres Inn
just a little ways down the street.

You mean you all live in a motel room?

Yes.

Can't you get assistance, like food stamps,
that sort of thing?

I don't qualify, that's what they told me,
anyway I don't want a hand
out, we make it OK.

Isn't the Acres the place
that just was cited by the Health Department?

Yeah, we got rats, roaches, you try not
to think about it, stay outta their way.

Will you have enough to pay
off the loan when it comes due?

Prob'ly not, it's alright, I'll
roll it over like usual.

But you keep paying
and doesn't the interest just add up?

I don't have no choice, I wanna have
a place for us—we gotta live.

That's all the time we have,
I'm Harriet Ashbury reporting for WNTV, now
back to the newsroom for your local weather.

The Conspiracy Surrounding The 2016 Word Of The Year

They sat at a table
outside of Clary's Café
the free lance journalist
and the book editor of
the New World Post.
It was early in the morning
the literary buffs who visit
Savannah usually show up
after noon to see the place
featured in Berendt's Midnight
in the Garden of Good and Evil
so it was mainly a few locals eating
breakfast fare hot buttered grits
and the house special egg
concoction hoppel poppel.

"The Morning News squashed
my story. Too sensitive right now.
My source is reliable. She says the word
was number one in searches. She says
Merriam-Webster got a call,
I quote her in the piece:
'Pick something else, we don't
care how you get it done' that's what
they were told to do. So
they put out that tweet begging
people to look up other words.
It's a cover-up for sure.
'Surreal' trumps 'fascism'
no way."

Real Fake News

> "how is it to be told? . . . in detailing the facts themselves?"
> Charles Reznikoff, Reznikoff Papers Box VII, Folder 26

@ChicagoDailyNews
"Terrible crimes are being committed,
we are not safe anywhere anymore,"
says Thomas Paine, Ward 16 Alderman.
@ElPasoTopNews
Joining Antifa is now illegal
punishable by 15 years in prison.
@CamdenCityNews
New Jersey couple
set to testify against
Hillary Clinton
killed in an explosion.
@Seattle_Post
Senate Democrats call for
Supreme Court nominees
to ignore the U.S. Constitution.
@SelmaDailyRebel
Waters: "SCOTUS pick
should be illegal immigrant."
@Anchorage_Times
"We don't need
U.S. farmers anymore,
we have grocery stores,"
says Canada's prime minister.
@TheSanFranciscoGoldenEra
Robert De Niro involved in a
child sex trafficking ring.
@BaltimoreNewsAmerican
Anthony Bourdain killed
by Clinton operatives.
@TheBrooklynEagle

Pope Francis Orders
White Women to Breed
with Muslims
@NewYorkLedger
Studies and research carried out
so far have proven that there is no reason
to believe that the Holocaust ever occurred.

From 2014 on, the Russians have set up numerous Twitter accounts in the name of defunct or non-existent news sources to deliver factual local news and have built up staunch follower bases in the process; then during an election cycle they become "operational" and spread false stories to influence voter opinion. The skill and bravado, not to speak of the success, of this form of cyber-warfare is most vexing and must somehow be countered. I selected some names referenced in the reports about this, augmented with others garnered from a Wikipedia list of defunct media, and paired these with stories scrutinized in Snopes.comit's all untrue, including the name of the Chicago Alderman. In selecting the name Thomas Paine, I had in mind the one who wrote a pamphlet originally to be titled Plain Truth, which spoke of the threat of tyranny in his time.

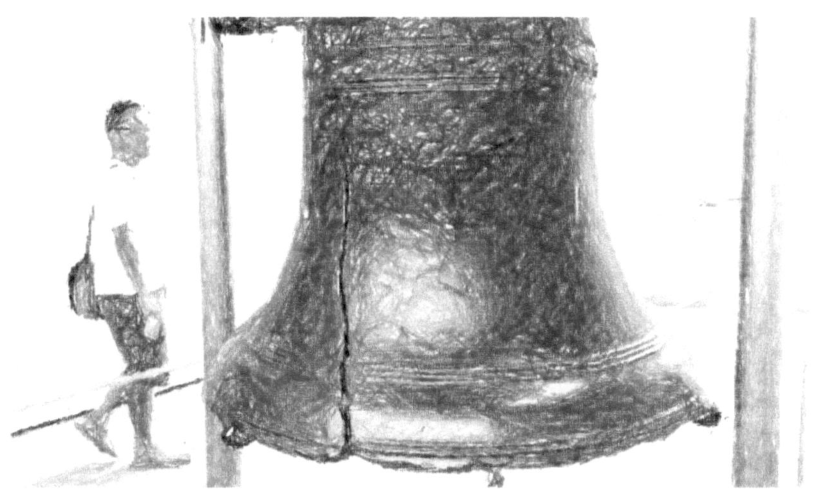

On Reading About The Lost Poetry Of The Angel Island Detention Center

My name doesn't matter. I am a Jew.
I was in Auschwitz. I was ten then.
I survived a death march.
I was liberated from another
concentration camp. I made it to
America on a Liberty ship crowded
with refugees. I came
through Ellis Island.
I don't want to talk about
any of thatI want to
talk about the poems. Poems
written in classic Chinese
style scratched on the walls
of a different place
across from Alcatraz
overlooking San Francisco Bay. I took
a sightseeing boat on
a visit there once, the tour guide
did not mention this. Now
I know. It opened in 1910
processing cases of Chinese laborers
under the exclusionary
laws of the 1880s, the first of its kind
in America sparked by a
post-Civil War recession in
which politicos and
opportunists portrayed the
Chinese as undesirables
depriving Americans of jobs.
They still came,
to *Gam Saan*
the Golden Mountain and

they waited to know their fate.
The detainees, held there for weeks
or months left disheartened verse behind:

I heard I was forbidden to land
I could do nothing but frown
and feel angry at heaven

pained words:

Today, we brothers are
imprisoned in a jail; it is
only because of our ancestral land

anguished words:

I am like pear blossoms which have
already fallen; pity the bare branches
during the late spring

defiant words lost in translation:

When I am idle, I have this wild dream
that I have gained the western barbarian's
consent to enter America

these vestiges of desperation all heroically saved
as was I, to stand witness to
humanity's inhumanity.

Credit for italicized sections: Lai, Him Mark, Genny Lim, and Judy Yung, eds. Island: Poetry and History of Chinese Immigrants on Angel Island, 1910-1940 © 1991. Reprinted with permission of the University of Washington Press.

Drumbeat

It started with the "Black Hebrew Israelites," that is the
group's name, shouting epithets at the boys
there before the Lincoln Memorial in the country's capital.
No, it started in 1970 when four demonstrators
were killed by troops trying to quell a Vietnam War
protest at Kent State University in Ohio.
No, it started in 1964 when three
civil rights workers two white, one black
were murdered in Mississippi by an angry mob.
No, it started in 1942 with the internment in California
and elsewhere of Japanese Americans during World War II.

It started in 1890 with the
slaughter of some say 250 Sioux at Wounded Knee
it started with the beating of a drum.

It started with the boys taunting the Omaha tribe elder
there, beating his drum, singing his chants.
No, it started in June of 1969 with the police raid
on the Stonewall Inn in New York City.
No, it started in 1919 with the lynching
of 237 black sharecroppers in Arkansas.
No, it started in 1913 when Leo Frank, a Jew,
was wrongly tried in Atlanta for the murder
of Mary Phagan and later died at the hands of vigilantes.
No, it started in 1865 with the rise of the Ku Klux Klan
marauding through the South, killing as they went.

It started in 1863 when 280 Shoshone men,
women and children were slaughtered
during the Bear Creek Massacre in Idaho
It started with the beating of a drum.

It started…
with the beating of a drum.

The incident to which this poem relates is the confrontation between a teenage student and a Native American elder. The story is encapsulated in the already iconic photo depicting the two protagonists facing each other, a breath apart, each standing their ground, each in their own way. The picture is a visualization in part of hatred, but so too of a kind of fear of the otherness of another, a juxtaposition of alterity that must be viewed as the latest in a line of such behavior which goes very far back in time. Explanations have been attempted, about the psychology of it all, trying to fathom it all, without much thought as to how to resolve it all. It is the stuff of which genocides are fueled, those that have come before and those occurring as this is being written, not to mention those that are yet to come.

Indigenous

(with selections adapted from The Gospel of the Redman, compiled by Ernest Thompson Seton)

No one owns the land
it all reverts to the tribe
no one owns the woods
of the forests, or the waters
of the rivers, this is the
way of the *native* Americans
wanzi oyate - one nation
pick no more berries than needed
avoid injuring anything which bears fruit
kill no more game than your camp requires
when you build a fire use only the fuel
you must and before moving on
extinguish the flame with care.
This is the way of the *native* Americans
wanzi oyate - one nation
it is at no time right to set
the forest afire, that is a lasting
calamity to all who dwell there,
the forest never recovers of
itself from such damage
let not cold, hunger, pain, or fear
of the very jaws of death itself
prevent you from doing a good deed.
This is the way of the *native* Americans
wanzi oyate - one nation
no one owns the soil of the earth
that soil is not ordinary soilit is
the dust of the blood, the flesh,
the bones of ancestors
the *native* Americans
bled and died to keep;

the land is their blood,
their dead, it is consecrated.
The eagle that sees afar sits in
the summit of the tree to watch
to the North and the South
and the East and the West
the eagle will scream and give
the alarm and come to the
front—wanzi oyate.

Selections adapted from The Gospel of the Redman used with permission, World Wisdom, Inc. The protest which took place regarding the Dakota Access pipeline has so many applicable ramifications to our times. The matter of what constitutes the collective good, the need for a reawakening of a sense of unity in this country, not to mention environmental issues all warrant our appreciation of the Native American perspective as exemplified in their effort, in consort with others like minded, to "listen to the land." Yes, jobs were at stake, and economic issues; it should be noted, it is the path this pipeline took, as much as the pipeline itself that is the issue. I have long greatly respected Native American values, as enunciated in one of my prized personal possessions an early copy of The Gospel of the Redman given to me as a gift over fifty years ago by my lifelong friend James Dunham, Native American expert, now Special Projects Director for the Booth Western Art Museum. I thought it was only fitting to try to express some of the fundamental thinking that surely must inform the action of those "spearheading" this extraordinary initiative. I strongly felt I needed to "spread the word" yet I felt as strongly that I could not presume to speak for the Native Americans involved, so I went to a classic source for their own words which I adapted to my purposes. Shortly after my writing this piece, President Obama ordered work to stop on a section of pipeline in contention pending further environmental studies, and shortly after that the courts halted construction on another section of the Dakota Access pipeline.

The Thimble Is Gone, What Next?

Monopoly's thimble token
is gone, removed from its
station as an original piece
by 4 million misinformed
votes of citizens without

respect for the value of
institutions, those who do not
recognize the merits of
retaining the pillars of
a game synonymous
with life itself; they
do not know that
the thimble is a symbol;
because they have not
taken time or do not care
to learn the history of this
hoary tiny shield which
provides a much needed
mantle of protection for
it guides the needle while
guarding the thumb,
in its time it served
other honorable purposes
as well, to measure spirits,
and gunpowder, for which
"just a thimbleful" would do;
over time thimbles attained
great value, a Meissen porcelain
version once brought $18,000 at a
Christie's auction, and in time of
war in England those who could
give nothing more donated their

silver thimbles which were melted
down for other valiant purposes,
the game's thimble should be
venerated and upheld, not dispatched
consider if we denigrated
other bulwarks of society in
like fashion, think about
the consequences
which could be wrought by
a similar plebiscite of ignorance.

Survival Of The Fittest

The aid which we feel impelled to give to the helpless is
mainly an incidental result of the instinct of sympathy.
—Charles Darwin, The Descent of Man

She is just
starting out in life
she is fed by a
machine breathes
with the aid of
another machine
take away the
machines, she dies.
She is on a bus driving
in darkness to reach
Washington D.C.
she is one of many
on that trek,
mothers, caregivers,
children and others
whose lives or loved
ones' lives hang in
the balance who live
because and only
because Medicaid
pays for their care.
The bus rolls on
in the dismal night,
it is a long and risky
flight for such fragile
souls as she. They
are on a mission, to plead
with those who hold
the future in their hands
to show the faces of

pending tragedy,
begging in favor of
reality vs. ideology.
She spikes a fever
on the way
there is trouble
with the feeding tube
her mother struggles
to provide some relief
as the hours pass
she barely improves,
exhausted they arrive
with the light of morning
at the place where
their appeal is intended.
They are barred from entry.
The office doors
are closed to them.
They are still hoping
to meet with their
congressman.

Before Hanukkah, 2018

Hanuka candle dances warm
To help you weather your heavy storm
Shines like my lighthouse light this night
to bring your worried soul my light
                    —From "Hanuka's Flame" by Woody Guthrie, 1949

On the one hand…
On October 27th, at the Tree Of Life
synagogue while sabbath
morning services ensue
a crazed gunman, a Jew-hater
kills eleven injuring seven in Pittsburgh.
On October 31st, the owner of
a kosher-style eatery
in Austin finds out the windows of
his food truck have been smashed to
smithereens, an Iron Cross ominously
left amidst the debris.
On November 4th at Harvard Square
in Cambridge a 66-year-old Jewish woman
is accosted her attacker putting his
fist on her throat, pushing her,
shouting hateful words.
On November 14th during a performance
of "Fiddler on the Roof" at the
Hippodrome Theatre in Baltimore
a man calls out "Heil Hitler" panicking
many who flee in fear.
On November 29th, the office
of a Jewish professor at Columbia University
in New York who writes about the Holocaust
is vandalized, virulent graffiti
and swastikas spray painted on the walls
On the other hand…

On November 27th, at around 9:30 p.m.
a fire of yet unknown origin breaks out
in the sanctuary at Congregation
Torah Vachesed in Houston, as dozens
of evening service worshippers rush to
escape, firefighters and police run into
the building and rescue every single
sacred Torah scroll, bringing them
all out, safe and sound.
On December 2nd, as darkness falls in
Kankakee, one of its few remaining
Jewish residents will place his menorah
in the window for all to see and
light one small candle, for eight nights in all,
to keep the flame of memory and truth ignited.

Tevye's monologue in "Fiddler on the Roof" invokes the Jewish life philosophy "on the other hand." There is always "the other hand." In an old tale which tells of coming doom when the world will succumb to a second flood, the rabbi goes to his people and says: "Jews, we have to learn to live under water." Deborah E. Lipstadt, professor of Holocaust history at Emory University whose win at trial against a Holocaust denier in England was portrayed in the 2016 movie "Denial" sums it up this way in a New York Times article "I'm not a Chicken Little who's always yelling, 'It's worse than it's ever been!' But now I think it's worse than it's ever been." She's talking about America. It's time to pick a side. Elie Wiesel makes it clear: "We must take sides. Neutrality helps the oppressor, never the victim. Silence encourages the tormentor, never the tormented." Ergo, the poetry of bearing witness.

All American

We headed up Florida's Turnpike,
passed by Sebring, remembering
the racetrack, one of the oldest
around, what most people don't know
in World War II it was an airfield
where Flying Fortress pilots trained
then a fellow named Ulmann
came along, converted the runways
To a raceway, endurance was the
mainstay, hosted the U.S.' first
Formula One like the European
Grand Prix; passed by Orlando
where a guy who drew a cartoon
mouse created what he imagined
could be a new world, E.P.C.O.T.
"Experimental Prototype Community
of Tomorrow" now called Disney World;
passed by Valdosta, where cotton was
king before the time of the Civil War
and after until the boll weevil came
calling down south then the town
reinvented itself with turpentine,
it's Friday night lights there too,
voted an ESPN "Titletown USA"
passed by Tifton, where the Peanut
Growers Association once sponsored
The Peanut Butter Lovers of America,
passed by Macon, thinking of
peaches and pecans--
on to Atlanta, the hub of the Southeast,
passed by the alpha city's skyline,
ragtag parts of town, palatial neighborhoods
scented with Margaret Mitchell's
Gone With the Wind, just making it thru

the gates of the cemetery in time
for the funeral. Uncle Bill Rubin
passed away at 91. He started life in Cleveland;
an orphan, a navy man, an engineer's
mind, a salesman's savvy, a heart
of gold, he worked his way from stock boy
to Swank VP big in the menswear industry
in his day he notched his belt with
boxing, tennis, golf trophies, accolades from
the myriads he befriended, helped, hosted with his
display of Midwest mixed with southern charm,
in boardrooms and dining rooms from
New York to California; sharing space
alphabetically in the Journal-Constitution obituaries,
taking his leave on the same weekend another
Atlanta staple, Joe Rogers, co-founder of Waffle House;
at 97 he fittingly died after having dinner with his wife;
the diner chain a veritable meeting place for
late-niters and early-risers, the hoity-toity
and the hoi polloi; we had a good eight hours driving
back going straight through the night without extra
stops, but those iconic signs kept passing by,
it was meant to be; we sat on stools
at the counter, spectators to the short order grill-man
and waitresses working their wonders, Cheese N' Eggs,
Steak & Eggs, City Ham, Country Ham, Hashbrowns
capped and smothered, Bacon Lover's B.L.T.
hold the mayo; Joe Rogers had the idea, Bill Rubin too
it's not about the food, it's about the people.

Oh, say does that star-spangled banner yet wave
O'er the land of the free and the home of the brave?—Francis Scott Key

"The Star-Spangled Banner" is the national anthem of the United States. The lyrics come from the "Defence of Fort M'Henry" a poem written on September 14, 1814, by the then 35-year-old lawyer and amateur poet Francis Scott Key after witnessing the bombardment of Fort McHenry by British ships of the Royal Navy in Baltimore Harbor during the Battle of Baltimore in the War of 1812. Key was inspired by the large U.S. flag, with 15 stars and 15 stripes, known as the Star-Spangled Banner, flying triumphantly above the fort during the U.S. victory. [excerpt from Wikipedia article]

James Dunham sketch of author in his salad days

Howard Richard Debs received a University of Colorado Poetry Prize at age 19. After spending the past fifty plus years in the field of communications, with recognitions including a Distinguished Achievement Award from the Educational Press Association of America, he resumed his creative pursuits. Debs is a recipient of the 2015 Anna Davidson Rosenberg Poetry Awards. His essays, fiction, and poetry appear internationally in numerous publications; His photography will be found in select publications, including in Rattle online as "Ekphrastic Challenge" artist and guest editor. His book Gallery: A Collection of Pictures and Words, is a 2017 Best Book Awards and 2018 Book Excellence Awards recipient. He is co-editor of New Voices: Contemporary Writers Confronting the Holocaust forthcoming in 2021 from Vallentine Mitchell of London, publisher of the first English language edition of the diary of Anne Frank. Born and bred in Chicago, he now lives in sunny South Florida with his wife of 55 years Sheila, where they spend considerable time spoiling their four grandchildren. He is listed in the Poets & Writers Directory: https://www.pw.org/content/howard_debs

The span from beginning to end is made from all that lies between